THE DONKEY GANG

BY BRIAN OGDEN

ILLUSTRATED BY ALAN HUNT

By the same author:
Long Trunk Short Tales
Garth the Giraffe
Henry and Hoppit
Published by The Leprosy Mission International

The Donkey Gang
Published by The Leprosy Mission International 2006

Edited and distributed by TLM Trading Limited,
The Leprosy Mission's trading company,
P.O.Box 212
Peterborough PE2 5GD
Phone: 0845 1662253 Fax: 01733 239258
Email: enquiries@tlmtrading.com
Further purchases can be made from: www.tlmtrading.com

Editorial and design by Creative Plus Publishing Ltd.
2nd Floor, 151 High Street, Billericay,
Essex, CM12 9AB
www.creative-plus.co.uk

Printed and bound in China
Phoenix Offset
A catalogue record for this book is available from the British Library
ISBN 0 902731 62 9

CHAPTER 1

MAJOR PROBLEMS

The donkey arrived in September. For weeks the field had been empty, but then so had the house next to it. Not long after Major Tangled-Hairpiece moved in (to the house not the field) the donkey arrived. The Major, it seemed, had worked with donkeys in his army days and had grown very fond of them. The Major, although still very upright, was now in his eighties.

"Much more sensible than humans, don't you know!" he was heard to say in the Post Office. But then a lot of things were heard in the Post Office. Being a military man, the Major called the donkey Captain. The Post Mistress asked why the donkey was called Captain. "Second-in-Command, don't you know," came the reply. "And a most valuable ass-istant." Captain 'what' nobody knew – it just seemed to be Captain.

Did you know that ass is another word for donkey? How many words beginning with ass can you find in this story?

The Major lived by himself in the house he re-named El Alamein, which came as rather a shock to the village as it had previously been named Rose Cottage. El Alamein was a very famous battle in the North African desert in the Second World War. Captain lived by himself in the field, though there was an old shed in one corner where he sheltered when the wind blew from the north.

The Major had never forgotten his army days and his mornings, despite his being 84 years old, always began the same way.

(It gets rather boring after this, so let's get on with the story.)

At first there were no problems – the Major was happy in El Alamein Cottage and Captain was happy in his field. The trouble began with children. It often does! The Major didn't like children, because unlike the big guns he was used to, children frightened him.

They didn't stand to attention when he spoke to them, their shoes were always dirty and most of them needed a haircut.

One day the Major happened to be driving past the field at 20 minutes past three. Five minutes later he would not have worried, ten minutes later he would have carried on driving, but at quarter past three the children came out of school. Five minutes later they were walking past the field.

"I wonder if he's hungry?' said Holly. "I've got a cheese sandwich left – let's see."

Holly, George and Amy are cousins who live in the same village and go to the same school. Holly is in Year 5 while George and Amy are in Year 4. Holly's mum called them The Gang.

Holly opened her sandwich box and held the crumbled bits of bread over the fence. Captain, never one to miss a nice snack, ambled over, and peeling back his lips in the way that donkeys do, bit deep into the sandwich. It was good. It was very good. Captain looked hard at Holly to see if there was anymore.

"I've got a jam roll," said George. "I'll give him that."

Captain was disappointed with the roll but ate it just the same. A sensible donkey does not look a gift human in the mouth. A car drew up just as Amy was emptying some ready-salted crisps into the field. It was the Major. By the time he had wound down the car window the children were disappearing round the corner into the wood on the edge of Captain's field. The Major waved his fist at the children and drove home.

The next day, on their way to school, Holly, George and Amy saw that the Major had put up a notice in the field.

As they stopped to read the notice Captain came trotting over to them.

"Well, he hasn't read the notice," said Holly laughing. "He's hoping we've got something for him."

The next week was half-term. The Major, not understanding schools and holidays, didn't realise that the children would be around all day. The Gang met on Monday morning in Holly's garage.

"If we go through the wood we can get right up to the fence and talk to Captain in a place where old Hangled-Tearpeace can't see us!" said Holly thinking aloud. "Donkeys are vegetarians, so we must be careful what we feed him."

"Has anyone got any carrots or apples?" asked Amy. "Captain would love them."

"I know where there are millions of apples," said George. "Steve, our neighbour, has an orchard. His shed's full of them."

"I hope Captain likes apples," said Amy quietly, "or they might make him ill."

"Of course he will," shouted Holly. "All donkeys like apples!"

"And when did you become an expert on donkeys?" asked George.

"When I looked them up on the Internet yesterday!" retorted Holly. "Let's try him with an apple and if he doesn't like that we'll find some carrots."

The children ran off to the apple packing shed. Although it was the end of October the weather was fine and the sun was shining. The shed was full of boxes of apples.

"Told you there were millions," said George with pride. "Steve sells apples for Christmas. They're called Coxes. He says I can always help myself."

"Coxes in boxes!" said Amy.

"Never mind what they're called," said Holly, "just grab a few quickly!"

They took a couple each and ran off across the farmyard before following the path through the wood towards the edge of Captain's field. They were pushing carefully past a thick holly bush covered with red berries when Holly stopped suddenly in her tracks.

"Major alert! Lie down!" whispered Holly dropping to the ground. The other two fell on top of her.

"Get off," she said pushing George into the bush.

"OUCH!" screamed George with holly leaves sticking in his legs.

"Well done George," said Holly angrily. "Now everyone knows we are here."

Fortunately the Major, who was feeding Captain with some carrots, was a little deaf.

"Comes of being in the Artillery, don't you know," he told the Post Mistress. "Deafened by all that gunfire!"

The Major did not hear George's yell, but Captain heard it loud and clear. The donkey did what we all do when we hear a loud noise. He suddenly lifted his head in the air to see where it was coming from. Major Tangled-Hairpiece, carrot in hand, couldn't get out of the way in time. Captain's head struck the Major's chin a swift blow and the donkey did for the Major what no enemy had achieved in six years of war. He knocked him out. The Major slid to the ground as Captain stood over him looking rather surprised at what he had done.

"Oh no! Now what do we do?" whispered Amy.

CHAPTER 2

AN AMBULANCE AND LOTS OF APPLES

Holly stood up, parted the branches in front of the fence, and looked into the field. Captain was standing quite still while the Major was lying flat on his back and out for the count. From where she was hiding Holly could see blood on the Major's face.

"We must get help," said Holly to the others. "George, use your mobile and phone for an ambulance. I'm going into the field to keep Captain from treading on the Major."

Holly pushed her way through the bushes and nettles. She climbed over the rusty metal fence, took out one of the apples, and walked very slowly towards the donkey holding out the apple in her hand. Captain trotted carefully round the Major and came over to Holly. George yanked his mobile phone from his jeans' pocket.

"What should I dial?" he shouted.

Captain stopped and looked.

"999 of course," said Amy, "and ask for the ambulance. We did it in Brownie Guides. You have to tell them exactly where we are."

Holly took a small step towards the donkey and held out the apple again. Captain took the apple and then looked for another one. There was a loud groan from the Major and Captain gave an ear-splitting HEE-HAW. This time it was Holly's turn to leap in the air.

Within ten minutes the children could hear the ambulance and see the flashing blue lights in the distance. It stopped and two paramedics jumped out to help.

"Over here," shouted Holly trying not to frighten Captain.

The paramedics looked at Captain and then slowly pushed open the gate. Major Tangled-Hairpiece groaned again and tried to sit up. He put his hand on the ground to push and shouted as a sharp pain ran up his arm.

The paramedics lifted the Major onto a stretcher and wheeled him off towards their ambulance. Holly followed and caught up with the Major just before the door was closed.

"Don't worry, Major," she said, "we'll look after Captain."

"Thank you," replied the Major in a frail voice. "I'd really appreciate that."

The children stood and watched as the ambulance drove off with the blue lights flashing. Captain looked very puzzled by the hee-hawing coming from the ambulance. It sounded like no other donkey he'd ever met. He followed the sound as it gradually faded, shook his head, and came to see if there were any more apples.

"We don't know anything about keeping donkeys," said Amy, looking worried.

"We had a budgerigar once," said George, scratching his head.

"I don't think that's quite the same thing!" said Holly, laughing. "We'd better look in the shed and see what he eats. I don't suppose a donkey is very different to a horse and I did have riding lessons on holiday last year."

They crossed over the field followed by Captain. Just outside the shed was an old tin bath tub.

"My Nan's got one like that," said Amy.

In the bottom of the bath some leaves and twigs, fallen from the over-hanging trees, were swimming around. Round the edge was a layer of green slime. Hopping about on the twigs was a large green frog.

"Right, first job is to fill that up so Captain can have a drink," said Holly. "Grab that bucket George – the tap's behind the shed."

"The first thing to do," said Amy, "is to rescue the frog."

"Well, that's your job," said Holly as she disappeared into the shed.

"She doesn't like frogs!" said George, as he cupped the frog in his hands and watched it hop off.

"Come and see what I've found," shouted Holly.

Amy went into the shed and found Holly standing staring at something poking out from a pile of straw.

"Whatever is it?" she asked.

"It's a saddle and reins and what not," whispered Holly. "Do you realise what this means?"

Amy looked puzzled. There was obviously something on Holly's mind but then she was used to her cousin having strange ideas. It was always better to let Holly answer her own questions.

"It means," said Holly with a big grin, "we have got a donkey and a saddle for our Nativity Play!"

The Major was kept in hospital for a week. During that time the children made sure that Captain had plenty to eat and fresh water to drink.

On the Friday of half-term the children met as usual by Captain's shed. Holly was carrying a plastic bag. Whilst the other two fed and watered Captain, Holly disappeared into the shed. Some minutes later she came out wearing a riding hat and carrying the harness, reins and saddle. The leather was gleaming, the straps were shining, and the buckles sparkled in the sun.

Amy and George were not the only ones to see the saddle. Captain took one look and trotted off as fast as he could.

"Apples!" said Holly. "George, we need apples and lots of them."

George ran off to Steve's shed muttering to himself about bossy girls giving orders. He came back, undid the zip on his fleece, and a whole pile of apples tumbled on the floor. Captain, not one to miss an apple when he saw it, came closer.

It would take too long to describe what happened next but it included Captain eating far too many apples, a saddle and a very bruised Holly. After picking herself up from the ground for the seventh time, she at last persuaded Captain to let her ride a short distance.

At break-time, in school the following Monday, the children knocked on the staff room door.

"Please may we speak to Mrs. Foster?" they said together.

The head teacher came to the door with a cup of coffee in her hand.

"We... err," said Holly, "we've got something really exciting to tell you."

"We've found a donkey and we want to use it...," said George in a rush.

"...in the Nativity play," added Amy.

"Thank you," said Mrs. Foster. "I'll think about it."

"That's the trouble with teachers," muttered Holly as they walked away, "they're always thinking about things. It usually means they won't do it."

But Holly was wrong. As school ended Mrs. Foster asked Holly to find out if Major Tangled-Hairpiece would let Captain take part in their play.

"Wait until the Major is home from hospital before you go," said Mrs Foster. "If he agrees, I'll send a note to your parents too, just to check that they're happy. Your Mum can ride, can't she Holly? I think we might need her help and advice!"

Later that week Holly, George and Amy went to visit the owner of El Alamein Cottage. They rang the bell and waited.

"I wonder what he will say?" said Amy.

"He was cross with us when we gave Captain those sandwiches!" said George.

Holly opened her mouth to speak. At that moment there was a very loud bang and what seemed like hundreds of pigeons flew screeching out of the trees.

"Vermin! That's what you are!" the voice echoed down the corridor of El Alamein Cottage.

"That was a gun!" said a somewhat shocked and shaken Holly.

CHAPTER 3

A DONKEY IN CHURCH

As the gunshot died away the children could hear footsteps coming towards the door. All three took several steps back.

"Did he call us vermin?" whispered Amy, still shaking.

The door opened and there stood the Major with a shot gun in his right hand and his left arm in a white hospital sling.

"Well don't just stand there! Come in," he bellowed.

The children followed him slowly into El Alamein Cottage. On every ledge and cupboard were mementos of the Major's time in the army.

There were photographs of famous generals, a case full of medals and a painting of donkeys crossing a desert with big packs on their backs.

"Glad you came," said the Major. "Wanted to thank you for fetching the ambulance. And old Captain... Well, he's very grateful too."

"Major," said Holly, "we have come to ask if we could borrow Captain."

"Borrow the old boy?" he said looking puzzled. "Whatever do you want a donkey for?"

"Christmas is coming," said Amy, "and we want Captain to carry Mary in our Nativity play."

Major Tangled-Hairpiece thought about it. The children held their breath.

"Yes, Captain would like that. But only if you," he said pointing to Amy, "are the one to ride him. You're the lightest. Captain isn't *ass* young *ass* he used to be."

You can imagine what the next three weeks were like. Amy spent almost as much time lying on the ground beside Captain as she did riding on top. But, with two or three riding lessons from Holly's mum, slowly and surely the donkey and Amy became friends. Then, with Holly holding the halter rein, Captain generally went where they wanted.

The school rehearsed their carols. The shepherds, the innkeepers and the wise men practised their parts, and Mrs Foster and the Vicar discussed the play.

"I am a little concerned about having a donkey in church," said the vicar, whose name was Canon Shotte.

"I understand," said Mrs Foster, "but he does help the story come to life."

"Not too lively, I hope," said the Vicar.

The dress rehearsal was a dreadful donkey disaster. Holly let go of Captain's halter for just a moment. The donkey spotted the huge vase of flowers standing on the font and munched his way through the lot. Then, as if to tell everyone what he had done, he gave an ear-splitting HEE-HAW, turned around and knocked a huge pile of hymn books flying. Fortunately, the vicar had been called away and missed all the fun!

Two days later the church was packed for the performance. More and more people kept pushing into the pews – there were grannies and granddads, aunts and uncles, dads and mums and a sprinkling of younger brothers and sisters.

Mrs Foster welcomed everybody and the play started with a carol. Holly, who was in the churchyard with Captain, saw the Major creep into the back of the church. As the carol ended, Amy, who was playing the part of Mary, came onto the stage. She looked suitably surprised when an angel came to tell her she was to have a very special baby. "He will be called the Son of God," said the angel.

The angel left and Mary was joined by Joseph, a tall, fifth-year boy called Sharif. To the sound of marching music, a Roman soldier marched up the aisle and announced:

YOU MUST ALL GO TO YOUR HOME TOWNS TO BE COUNTED!

That was the cue for Holly and Captain. Holly led the little donkey to the front of the church and Amy climbed carefully onto his back. Joseph walked by the side of Captain as they went first down, and then back up the aisle while the children sang 'Little Donkey'. Captain seemed to know that he was carrying somebody very important, even if it was only Amy. He behaved perfectly.

Mary and Joseph made their home in the stable and Captain stood guard by their side. Everyone sang, 'Away in a manger,' as Amy cradled a large baby doll. The younger children sang a song about the angels and the play continued with the shepherds visiting baby Jesus in the stable. Later the wise men brought their gifts for the baby King. In the last carol Holly took Captain's reins again. Mary sat on the donkey proudly holding her baby.

"Mary, Joseph and the baby Jesus went to Egypt," said the narrator, "to save Jesus from wicked King Herod."

As Holly led the procession back through the church to the door everyone started to clap. Captain, who had been quiet the whole time, thought he should join in and gave a very loud HEE-HAW.

Holly saw the Major walk out of the church. There were tears in his eyes and a smile on his lips.

"That, my dear," he said to Holly, "was a very special nativity play!"

CHAPTER 4

AND THE CROWDS CHEERED

On Christmas morning, The Gang met at Captain's field immediately after the morning service. They had wrapped up some Turkish Delight for the Major and brought special treats for the donkey too. George brought apples, Amy had some carrots and Holly some peppermints.

"Happy Christmas," said the Major, as he walked across the field towards them carrying three identical gift-wrapped parcels. "Thanks to you three it's been one of me best." The children unwrapped their presents and discovered three identical notebooks each with a picture of a donkey on the felt cover.

"It's a kind of Donkey Diary," said the Major. "Thought you might like to write about your adventures, draw a few pictures, that sort of thing."

"These are amazing!" said Amy. "I'm going to stick a photo of me playing Mary and riding Captain on the first page."

"Jolly good idea," beamed the Major. "I'm sure old Captain is still dreaming about treading the boards."

"He means being in the play," whispered Holly to the others.

"Don't suppose there'll be another chance," said the Major.

As Amy and George stroked Captain and fed him, Holly stood there thinking. There must be another chance for Captain. Something in her memory was saying 'donkey'.

But it was not until weeks later that Holly remembered why.

It was a cold start to the New Year – flurries of snow and icy puddles. Major Tangled-Hairpiece didn't like the cold weather.

"Comes of fighting in the desert, you know," he told the children. "Be really grateful if you would take care of Captain."

And so they did – on the way to school and on their way home, they fed Captain and topped up his water.

One morning, just after half term, Mrs Foster spoke to the children in assembly.

"In the next few weeks we shall be thinking about Easter. Our Christmas Play was so popular that Canon Shotte has invited us to do something special for Palm Sunday. If anyone has some good ideas please come and see me."

Without thinking, Holly put up her hand.

"Donkey, Miss!" she shouted.

Mrs Foster looked very cross.

"Come and see me after assembly, Holly Green!" she said.

Holly stood outside the head teacher's office. What had she done wrong now?

"I hope, Holly Green," said Mrs Foster still looking cross, "that you will apologise now for what you called me."

"I didn't call you anything," said Holly.

"Holly, I'm really disappointed with you. You definitely called out donkey."

"But Miss, it was my idea for Palm Sunday. We could use Captain, the donkey, in our Palm Sunday thing in church."

Mrs Foster began to smile and then she laughed loudly.

"It's I who should say sorry," she said. "That's a really good idea. Will you please ask the Major if we may borrow Captain again?"

On their way home the three children went round to El Alamein Cottage. Parked in the drive was a car that the children recognised.

"That's Doctor Watson's car," whispered George. "I hope the Major's all right."

At that moment, the doctor came out, jumped in his car, and drove off waving to the children. It took a long time for the Major to answer the door of El Alamein Cottage when the children knocked. He looked very pale. He was wrapped up in a thick army great coat, wore a khaki scarf round his neck and seemed to be shivering.

"Not feeling too good," he said coughing. "Doc says I must keep in bed."

"We'll look after Captain," said Holly, "and please may we borrow him once again?"

The Major coughed, smiled weakly and nodded his head as he turned and shut the door.

"Yes!" shouted Holly and punched the air. "We can use Captain in our Palm Sunday play."

The next morning the three children told Mrs Foster what had happened.

"That sounds really exciting," said the head teacher. "We can have a Palm Sunday procession with everyone in the school taking part. Mrs Wilkinson is going to write the play so you can tell her that we shall have a real donkey and I'm sure he'll be a real *ass-et* to the performance!"

After school they went to feed Captain. The old donkey didn't seem quite his usual self – he wasn't very interested in his food.

"Perhaps he's not feeling too well either," said George. "Perhaps he's feeling a little 'horse'. Maybe he needs some cough stirrup," he joked.

"I think he's just missing the Major," said Amy. "I hope he'll be all right for the play."

"Holly," said George as he poured water in the old tin bath, "I can't remember what happened on Palm Sunday. Why do we need a donkey?"

"Well," said Holly, "Jesus is grown-up now and it's near the end of his life. He sent two of his friends to borrow a donkey. When they brought it, he rode into Jerusalem on its back to show the crowds that he was coming in peace."

"And the crowds cheered," added Amy.

"And they waved palm branches... that's why it's called Palm Sunday," said Holly.

"I think it would be better," said Canon Shotte, "if you were to do the Palm Sunday procession outside the church and then come in for the service."

"I agree totally," said Mrs Foster, when the vicar spoke to her after taking the assembly. "I'm sure the children will enjoy it."

For the next three weeks every craft lesson was used to make palm branches and leaves. Some of the older children learned how to make big leafy palm crosses.

Meanwhile after school, George, who was the lightest boy in his class, was trying very hard to ride Captain. Holly put the saddle on the donkey and George stood on an old chair and tried to put his leg over the donkey's back. The problem was he didn't stop when he was on top – he just kept going and landed with a bump on the other side.

"I know Jesus was a man," said George, "but couldn't one of you ride Captain in the play?"

"No," said Holly, "Canon Shotte told Mrs Foster we must have a boy, and that's you."

Once again Holly's mum provided a few riding lessons and by Palm Sunday George was spending most of each ride in the saddle. On the day itself, all the children and adults lined up on either side of the road by Captain's field.

"Jesus asked two of his disciples to fetch a donkey," said Mrs Wilkinson, the narrator, as loudly as she could.

Holly and Amy, wearing biblical costumes, went into the field and led Captain out on to the road. Very carefully George, dressed as Jesus, climbed on, and with Holly holding the reins, they set off towards the church.

A man from the local paper took photographs while the children and adults cheered and waved palm branches. They also put some paper palm leaves down on the road to make a soft carpet for the donkey to walk on. Even when one of the palm leaves flew through the air and fell just in front of him, the old donkey behaved perfectly. At the church door, George climbed down from Captain's back and led the procession into the church.

"We're very fortunate," said Mrs Wilkinson, "to have Captain in our play again. Of course, the story of Palm Sunday continues with all that happened on Good Friday when Jesus was put on a cross to take the punishment for all our wrongdoing."

"Captain reminds us, not only of Palm Sunday, but also of Easter," she continued. "If you look carefully at a donkey's back, you will see two darker lines of fur that make a cross shape over his shoulders. It's an empty cross, which reminds us that Jesus came back to life again on Easter morning and is still alive today."

"I hope they put some good photos in the paper," said Holly, "I want a picture for my Donkey Diary."

As they went quietly back into the church they noticed someone rather special sitting right at the back. It was the Major. He looked much better than when they saw him last.

CHAPTER 5

HAPPY BIRTHDAY

It was mid May and the children had been back at school after the Easter holidays for several weeks. One day, as they were feeding Captain, they met the Major.

"I say," he said, "can you spare a mo? There's something rather important I want to say."

"I hope it doesn't mean we can't see Captain anymore," whispered George.

"Perhaps he's going away," said Amy.

The Major stood by Captain's shed smoking his smelly old pipe. He tapped it against the shed to empty out the tobacco ashes.

"You chaps...er... and chappesses have been jolly decent," he said, "the way you've looked after old Captain. It's me birthday – 85th actually – on Sunday. Rather hoping you might help me celebrate. I'll never blow out 85 candles on my own!"

It was then that Holly noticed a little curl of smoke coming from the straw beside Captain's shed. As she watched, it burst into flames. The wind blowing across the open field fanned the flames and in no time, more straw was alight.

Captain hee-hawed and trotted, terrified, to the other side of the field.

"Amy, take the Major away from the shed," shouted Holly. "George, grab your mobile and 'phone 999 for the fire brigade!"

Holly dashed into the shed and ran out carrying Captain's precious saddle. She walked slowly towards the donkey and tried to calm him down. The Major, Amy, George, Holly and Captain all lined up by the fence. They watched in horror as the wind blew the flames. Soon the whole shed was blazing. By the time the fire engine arrived all that was left was smouldering straw. Captain looked very puzzled. The fire engine sounded just like the ambulance when it had taken the Major to hospital. There were some very strange four-wheeled donkeys about, thought Captain, and he hee-hawed loudly.

The firemen hosed down the ashes, tidied up the straw, and drove off. Captain stood waiting for the strange hee-haw from the fire engine but this time it didn't come.

"What shall we do now?" said Amy, with tears in her eyes. "Captain is homeless."

"Seen worse in the war, my dears," said the Major. "Soon have another shed put up. What matters is that no humans or donkeys were hurt."

Canon Shotte came into school the next morning to take the assembly.

"Next Sunday," he said, "is a special day in the church's year. We call it Pentecost. Pentecost means 50th – it is the 50th day after Easter. Can someone tell me what happened to the friends of Jesus at Pentecost?"

"The Holy Spirit came," said George. "There was a strong wind and things like flames. Must have been really scary!"

"Thank you, George," said Canon Shotte. "I'm sure it was scary. Yes, there was the sound of a howling wind and what looked like fire. The friends of Jesus knew that something wonderful had happened. Before he went back to heaven, just after Easter, Jesus had promised they would get this special gift."

Amy nudged Holly.

"That's like yesterday," she whispered. "There was wind and flames."

Amy collected one of Mrs Foster's I-know-that-you-are-talking-stop-it-now looks.

"We call Pentecost the birthday of the church," Canon Shotte continued. "The Holy Spirit is a bit like an invisible helper. It gave Peter the courage to speak to the crowds in Jerusalem. Lots of them became Christians and that was how the church began. So the church celebrates its birthday at Pentecost."

"And the Major asked us to his birthday party," whispered Holly.

Luckily, one of the Reception class had started to cry and Mrs Foster didn't see Holly talking.

"Let's go and see the Major," suggested Holly on their way home. "He was telling us about his birthday when Captain's shed burnt down."

"I expect he's forgotten that," said George.

However, the Major had not forgotten. On Friday afternoon on their way back from school, the children stopped by Captain's field. Parked by the gate was a large lorry. On the side of the lorry they read the words, 'FRED'S SHEDS'.

Two men were in the field. They had put up the walls of Captain's new home and were just lifting the roof on. Captain kept his distance in one corner of the field, but he was watching what was going on with great interest.

On Sunday afternoon, Holly, Amy and George went to Captain's field. They had each made the Major a birthday card and had bought some birthday chocolates. Holly had also cut out the local paper's photo of Captain on Palm Sunday and put it in a smart wooden frame.

"So glad you could make it," said the Major. "Captain's new home is finished. Come and see."

The new shed was larger than the old one. It had windows on either side and a big barn door. The Major opened the door and there was the most amazing birthday spread The Gang had ever seen. Laid out on the bench next to Captain's stall was a huge birthday cake with one candle, and surrounding the cake were crisps, sausage rolls, dips, chocolate mini-rolls and *ass-orted* bottles of drink.

"Help yourselves," said the Major, laughing at the children's faces. "Anything left over goes straight to Captain!"

Holly's mum, the Post Mistress and several neighbours all dropped in for the birthday tea. After half an hour nobody could eat any more.

"Happy Birthday, Major," said Holly, sitting on an upturned bucket. "It's been a brilliant party."

"Yes," said Amy, "and all because there was a wind and then a fire. Now we've had a birthday as well."

"That's what happened on the first day of Pentecost," said George, "but they didn't have a donkey!"

At that moment there was a loud hee-haw and Captain appeared in the open door.

"I don't suppose that it's good for donkeys," said Holly, "but here's a piece of cake."

The donkey swallowed the cake whole and looked for more. "No more! Or you'll wind up in horse-pital with tummy ache!" joked Holly.

"Best birthday I've had in years," said the Major, laughing.

CHAPTER 6

MISSING!

Amy was the first to see what had happened. She was taking Sniff, the family dog, for a walk early one morning. It was three weeks into the summer holidays. It was already hot and she couldn't sleep. They walked down the path by the side of Captain's field with Sniff living up to his name. Sniff examined every hole, bush and tree he came across.

The path ended at the road and as Amy turned to walk along the pavement, she saw it. The gate in Captain's field was open. The field was donkey-less.

Amy and Sniff ran into the field. Captain had vanished. Perhaps he's *ass-leep* in his shed thought Amy. But the shed was empty – far too hot for a donkey in this weather. There was no sign of Captain anywhere.

Amy and Sniff, who really wanted to sniff around the field, ran as fast as they could to the Major's front door. Amy pushed the doorbell, knocked as hard as she could, and shouted at the same time. At last, Major Tangled-Hairpiece opened the door. Amy noticed porridge in his moustache and there were no shoes on his feet.

"Major," shouted Amy, "Captain's gone."

"Should be on parade in ten minutes," said the Major. "This is disgraceful. *Ass-went* without leave!"

"Major, you don't understand," yelled Amy almost in tears, "Captain's run away."

"Wait there," ordered the Major. He reappeared in two minutes wearing green wellies on the wrong feet.

Amy dragged a very unwilling Sniff away from all sorts of lovely new smells in the Major's garden. She and the Major walked as fast as they could to the field. The gate was still open and the field was still empty.

At that moment, Holly came cycling round the corner. She stopped when she saw the others.

"What's wrong?" she said.

"Captain has gone!" said Amy miserably. "Someone has left the gate open and he's run away."

"Right," said Holly looking very serious. "I shall look for him on my bike. Amy, why don't you take that sniffy dog home and get your bike too?"

"I think I should telephone the constabulary," said the Major looking very worried.

"I think Sniff might find Captain," said Amy. "He's a very clever dog really."

Holly looked rather doubtful that Sniff would turn into a bloodhound and pedalled off. The Major went back to El Alamein Cottage and Amy ran off with Sniff.

"Sniff, sniff!" she ordered the dog. Usually he was told not to sniff – now he was told to sniff. Humans can be very puzzling, thought the dog.

Holly went past El Alamein Cottage and past the Post Office towards the school. She asked everyone she saw if they had seen a donkey.

"No, you're the first!" shouted Jack and Terry, not very helpfully.

"Perhaps he has a secret *ass-ignation*!" suggested Sharif with a grin.

Amy and Sniff, no longer a scruffy mongrel but now a tracker dog, went off in the other direction. Sniff showed no interest in the path which they had come along earlier so Amy carried on towards the garage and the small housing estate.

"You want to report a what?" said the police officer.

"A donkey called Captain," said the Major.

"I hope sir, you're not trying to make an ass of the police?" came the reply.

"No I am not!" shouted Major Tangled-Hairpiece. "My donkey is missing."

The officer took a description of Captain and *ass-ured* the Major that the police would look out for him.

Meanwhile Holly had reached the end of the village and turned round to try somewhere else. Amy and Sniff looked in every garden on the estate, but there was no sign or sniff of Captain. The Major got out his car and drove round the village hoping to find his Second-in-Command.

After an hour, all three of the searchers met up by the open gate. Not one of them had caught a glimpse of the old donkey.

"It's hopeless," said Amy, "he's probably miles away by now."

"No one has seen him," said Holly.

"We'll have to leave it to the constabulary," said the Major with a very long face. "We'll see if there is any message back at base."

They walked back to El Alamein Cottage. As they opened the gate, Sniff went mad, barking and tugging on his lead.

Sniff dragged Amy round to the back garden.

There, eating the Major's lettuces, was a very contented Captain.

"See," said Amy triumphantly to her *ass-ociates*, "it was Sniff who found him! I'm going to write about this adventure in my Donkey Diary!"

CHAPTER 7

A SERGEANT, A CAPTAIN AND A MAJOR

Captain settled down again in his field after his adventures. The long summer holiday came to an end (sadly, it always does) and The Gang were on their way back to school again.

"I wonder what the new teacher's going to be like?" said Amy as they passed Captain's field. The old donkey brayed loudly when he saw them.

"I shall know soon," said Holly. "He's taking my class!"

Mrs Foster introduced the new teacher to the whole school in Assembly.

"We are very pleased to welcome Mr Sergeant to our school and hope he will be happy here."

"Now we've got a major, a captain and a sergeant!" whispered Holly.

Amy started giggling. Mrs Foster stopped speaking and looked at both girls.

"I'm sorry Mr Sergeant. Amy and Holly come and see me at break time. Now, Mr Sergeant has just come back from teaching in Africa. I'm sure he will have a lot to tell us about that country later in the term."

Holly tried very hard not to be noticed in Mr Sergeant's first lesson. At break she joined Amy outside Mrs Foster's office.

"I am really disappointed with you both," said Mrs Foster. "I want you to go and apologise to Mr Sergeant for your behaviour in assembly."

They found Mr Sergeant and told him they were very sorry for laughing.

"Why was it funny?" he asked the two girls.

"Well," said Holly, "it's because we know a major and a captain and now we have a sergeant... er, a Mr Sergeant."

"Captain is a donkey who's been in our school plays," added Amy.

"I'd like to meet your Captain," said Mr Sergeant smiling at the girls. "You see I got to know a lot of donkeys in Africa. They are amazing animals."

Three days later, after school, Mr Sergeant met The Gang together with Major Tangled-Hairpiece at Captain's field. The old donkey, expecting a treat, came over to the fence.

To everyone's surprise, including Captain's, Mr Sergeant took several carrots out of his pocket and offered them to the donkey.

Captain didn't mind strangers who grew carrots in their pockets and he and Mr Sergeant soon became friends. (And now, I'll let you into a secret. That was the beginning of the school's DONKEY HARVEST PROJECT.)

"It's fantastic finding a donkey on the doorstep," said Mr Sergeant. "At my school in Africa a lot of our children looked after their family's donkey. Donkeys can do so many things."

"Absolutely!" said the Major. "The finest animals on earth."

If donkeys could blush, Captain would have done so. As it was, he looked for another carrot.

Holly listened hard to what her teacher had said about donkeys in Africa. Something began to stir in her mind – there just might be another way of using Captain this term.

The Gang walked home from the field but before they separated, Holly stopped them.

“I’ve got a brilliant idea,” she said to the other two. “It’s Harvest Festival soon. What about saving up to buy a donkey for a family in Africa?”

The next morning Mrs Foster found The Gang waiting outside her office.

“Mrs Foster,” said Holly rather excitedly, “could we buy a donkey at Harvest?”

“Why on earth do we need a donkey?” asked Mrs Foster smiling.

“Not for us,” said George, “but for a needy family in Africa.”

“Mr Sergeant knows all about donkeys in Africa,” added Amy.

“Well, I think I had better have a word with Mr Sergeant,” said Mrs Foster. “Now back to the playground.”

“She didn’t say no,” said George.

“She didn’t say yes either,” said Holly.

Two days later Mr Sergeant asked Holly, Amy and George to meet him in the lunch break.

"Mrs Foster," he said, "has agreed to your idea of buying a donkey for the Harvest Project – if I will take charge of the fund-raising. I am only willing to do that if I am sure you will help."

Mr Sergeant looked at the three children in turn. Each one nodded their head.

"So that's a promise then," he said. "We will work together to buy a donkey for a family in Africa. I know about Africa, but you know about this school and this village. I want you to come up with some money-raising ideas before we meet again."

"But how much is a donkey?" asked Amy.

"We will need about £50 to buy one through a charity that can deliver the donkey to a needy family."

The Gang went home with Holly after school. They sat round the dining room table with the Donkey Diaries that the Major had given them at Christmas and a plate of chocolate cookies.

They wrote down all their ideas in a long list. After ten minutes and eleven chocolate biscuits they stopped.

(Lists get boring, so let's move on and see what actually happened.)

Mr Sergeant spoke to the whole school in assembly, telling them about Africa.

"Many families need donkeys for all sorts of reasons. Donkeys carry loads, they carry people, they pull carts, and they help to pump water to the fields and many other things. A donkey costs around £50 – that money will take the donkey to the people who need it and make sure it has the right vaccinations to keep it healthy."

"A donkey can make a very big difference," finished Mr Sergeant. "Will you help me to raise enough money to buy one to help a needy family in Africa?"

CHAPTER 8
NEW OWNERS

The school went donkey mad during the three weeks before Harvest. The Major agreed to let Holly's mum organise donkey rides round the field after school at 50p a time. Some of the children made cakes that they sold at break. Two teachers did a sponsored donkey diet and lost lots of weight eating very little other than carrots and apples. There was a sponsored wonky donkey race when the children raced on all fours. Some of the children gave up a month's pocket money. There was also 'Pin the tail on the Donkey' when everyone paid 10p to enter.

Although it was a long time before Christmas, all the children were invited to design a Christmas card, which had to have a donkey in the picture. The best was chosen, printed and sold.

There was a non-uniform wear-a-donkey-mask day for which everyone gave money.

Amy's mask was voted the best by the whole school.

At last, the time came for the Harvest Thanksgiving Service. The children sang harvest songs. Some of the children had written the prayers for the service. One thanked God for all the good things we have in this country. Another prayed that all the donkeys in the world would be cared for properly. Mr Sergeant told everyone a story about a guard donkey that kept wild animals away from ducks and chickens. The donkey hee-hawed so loudly that any wild animal ran away.

After the service came the moment everyone had been waiting for – the result of THE DONKEY HARVEST PROJECT.

It was quiet in the School Hall as Mrs Foster and Mr Sergeant walked on to the stage.

"You have all worked so hard," said Mrs Foster, "to help us buy a donkey for a family in Africa. Everyone has joined in. The cakes and donkey rides, the Donkey Dieting, and all the other things have gone really well. You have raised not £50, or even £100 but a total of £150!"

Mrs Foster's voice was drowned as the whole school clapped and cheered. When at last it was quiet, she spoke again.

"That means that three donkeys will be going to new homes – to three families who really need their help."

"Mrs Foster, may I please interrupt you?" asked Mr Sergeant. "I have an envelope here. In it there is a letter from Major Tangled-Hairpiece. This is what it says…"

Dear Mrs. Foster and Children,

When I came to the village, I made the mistake of wanting to keep children away from my donkey. Since then I have learnt that I was wrong. The children have done so much for me and for Captain.

As our way of expressing our gratitude, I would ask you to accept a small cheque towards your Donkey Harvest Project.

Yours sincerely,

Albert Tangled-Hairpiece

Mr Sergeant held up the cheque.

"It is for £100," he said, "and that means we can buy two more donkeys."

"So our Harvest Festival will help to change the lives of not three but five families in Africa," said Mrs Foster. "Well done everyone."

Half term came and went, and soon the children were thinking about Christmas again.

Two or three weeks before the Nativity Play, The Gang went round to see the Major.

"I'm afraid I've got some news for you," said the Major. "My doctor tells me that I should not be living by myself any longer. I have a place in a Home for Retired Army Officers and shall be moving in after Christmas."

The children looked very sad as they went back down the path of El Alamein Cottage.

"We never asked about Captain," said Holly. "I mean he can't go with the Major."

"Perhaps the Major is going to sell him," suggested George.

"I don't think anyone would buy an old donkey," said Amy with tears in her eyes.

The Nativity Play went well and once again Captain behaved like a regular trooper.

On Christmas Eve, The Gang went round to take Captain and the Major their Christmas presents.

"I have a small present for you three," said the Major. "I have asked your parents and they have all agreed."

The children all looked at each other, wondering what it could be.

"Holly, Amy and George you are now the new owners of Captain. I couldn't wish for anyone else to look after him. You have been so kind to both of us and I know how much Captain looks forward to seeing you each day."

"Thank you so much!" said George happily.

"He'll be the best-kept donkey in the whole county!" said Amy. "We'll send you photos."

"I guess..." commented Holly, "that this makes us more than just The Gang. Let's call ourselves The Donkey Gang from now on!"